libraries ni

Please return this item by the date above.
You can renew it at any library, or via call-point
028 9032 7515, or online
www.librariesni.org.uk

CATNIP BOOKS
Published by Catnip Publishing Ltd
14 Greville Street
London EC1N 8SB

First published 2012
1 3 5 7 9 10 8 6 4 2

Text copyright © 2012 Margaret Ryan
Illustrations copyright © 2012 Sarah Horne

A CIP catalogue record for this book is available from the British Library.

ISBN 978-1-84647-144-5

Printed in Poland

www.catnippublishing.co.uk

ROODICA THE RUDE

Party Pooper!

MARGARET RYAN

Catnip

For Ross, with love

Long, long ago...

Back through the swirling mists of time when wolves and bears and wild boar roamed the land, and underpants hadn't been invented, the Romans throught it would be a 'superba idea' to invade Britain. The people of Britain, or Celts as they were then called, thought this was a rotten idea and fought back.

Thump! Thud! wallop! OUch!

But despite that, the Romans won.

(Romans 1 - Celts 0)

And the Romans stayed. They built fine houses and straight roads and taught washing, 'Don't forget to wash behind your ears, o stinkius peasant!'

They also collected taxes. Lots of taxes. King Bren of Brensland didn't like taxes or the Romans. He preferred going off to war. So he did. Trouble was, he left his wife, Queen Goodica, and their three daughters, Foodica, Woodica and Roodica behind to fend for themselves . . .

Roodica's Royals (The Celts)

King of Brensland

Likes fighting, fighting and fighting. Oh and wars, where he's usually to be found, right in the middle of the fighting.

Queen of Brensland

Likes peace and quiet. Lives at Maiden Castle trying to bring up her three daughters as proper princesses.

Princess Foodica

The eldest daughter and a proper princess. She's always neat and tidy, never says anything wrong, and is a wonderful cook.

Princess Woodica

The middle daughter and a proper princess. She's always sweet and gentle, never does anything wrong, and makes wonderful things out of wood.

Princess Roodica

The youngest daughter and a proper . . . pain in the posterior. She's never neat and tidy, never sweet and gentle, and is always saying and doing everything wrong. Her mother wonders what on earth she'll do with her.

Roodica's Friends

Fleabag, the wolfhound

He goes everywhere
with Roodica.

Plodette, the pony

She carries Roodica
around sometimes.
Slowly.

Gideon, the horse boy

He tries to keep Roodica
out of trouble.
Fat chance!

11

The Terrible Togas (The Romans)

Magnus Maximus (Big Max)

Very superstitious Roman governer. Likes ordering people about and getting presents. Wishes someone would hurry up and invent underpants as he finds Britain rather chilly.

MAGNUS MAXIMUS

FATIUS GUTTUS

Fatius Guttus (Fat Gut)

Tax collector (Boo hisss). Likes collecting taxes, taxes and more taxes, especially from those crummy Celts. Also likes eating, drinking and burping loudly.

Copius Mucus (Lottasnot)

Son of Fatius Guttus.
Likes telling tales,
sneaking up
on people
and sniffing.

COPIUS MUCUS

Roodica Plans a Party! Yippee!

It would soon be Roodica's birthday and in the big hall of Maiden Castle her sisters were trying to make her look like a proper princess for her party.

"Do sit still, Roodica, while I pick the twigs from your hair," said Foodica. "How did you manage to get them there? Were you playing soldiers in the woods with Gideon and Fleabag again?"

"No," giggled Roodica. "Fleabag and I

were having a game of wrestling and we
rolled and rolled all the way down the hill
and right through the settlement. It was
great fun."

Woodica sighed. "Well, *this* is not much
fun. Do stop wriggling while I try to
untangle these curls. Do you ever comb
your hair?"

"Every time I comb
Fleabag's," grinned
Roodica.

Foodica and Woodica looked over at the scruffy wolfhound snoozing quietly by the open fire. "That'll be never then," they muttered, and had another go at straightening Roodica's curls.

"OW, let go! You're pulling my head off!" yelled Roodica. "How can I have a birthday party with no head? How can I eat my birthday cake with no head? How can I sing 'Happy Birthday to me' with no head?"

"We're only trying to fix your hair in the latest style," said Foodica, tugging the bone comb through her tangles.

"And plaits are very fashionable," said Woodica, trying to wind one in a circle round Roodica's ear.

"But my hair doesn't want to be fashionable!" yelled Roodica. "It wants to be messy. It wants to be curly. Why can't you just leave it alone?"

"Do be quiet, Roodica," said her mother, Queen Goodica, coming to inspect her daughter's hair. "Your sisters are doing their best to make you look like a proper princess for your party and all you can do is complain. Foodica spent ages gathering stinging nettles to make thread and she has woven some beautiful cloth for your new dress."

"I know," muttered Roodica. "And it's really nice, but . . ."

"And Woodica spent ages making a little stool with a carved mouse on it to exchange for a bronze belt to go with the dress. She got Will the blacksmith to make the tiny bells to hang on the belt too."

"I know," muttered Roodica. "And it's really nice, but . . ."

"But what?" sighed the queen.

"When I invited all the settlement children to my birthday party, I promised I would have a kick-the-apple party."

"A kick-the-apple party?" The queen shuddered. "Oh, I don't think so . . . proper princesses don't have kick-the-apple parties . . ."

Roodica was about to protest when there was the sound of galloping hooves. They came to an abrupt halt outside Maiden Castle.

SQUAWK! SQUAWK! The castle ducks took fright and scattered in every direction.

"Who's upsetting the ducks?" frowned Roodica, and she escaped from the clutches of her sisters and ran to see.

A large Roman soldier stood in the doorway. He towered above Roodica, his vast bulk blotting out the sun.

"What do you want, helmet head?" she asked. "Have you come to tell us you're going back to your own country? Have you come to say goodbye? Well, *vale*. Goodbye and good riddance."

"Roodica, please don't be rude," said the queen, appearing at her side. "What can we do for you, centurion?"

"I was told to deliver this, ma'am," said the soldier, and he held out a rolled-up piece of parchment.

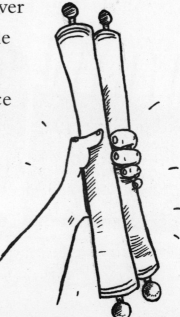

"Thank you," said the queen, and went back inside.

"Now **buzz off**," said Roodica to the soldier. "But buzz off slowly and don't scare the ducks this time."

The soldier looked down at her and gave a hard stare. Roodica looked up at him and made a horrible face.

"I can see right up your nose," she said. "And it's really hairy."

"Come inside, Roodica," called the queen, and she sat down by the big fire and unrolled the parchment.

Roodica, Foodica and Woodica gathered round to hear what it said.

"It's from Magnus Maximus, the Roman governor," said the queen.

"Big Max?" said Foodica. "What does he want?"

"Not more taxes, I hope!" said Woodica. "We've no money left to pay more taxes."

"The Romans are not really leaving, are they?" asked Roodica hopefully.

The queen shook her head. "No, it's nothing like that. It's an invitation to Magnus Maximus's birthday party."

"Another birthday party?" said Foodica. "Good thing I made you that frock, Roodica."

"Good thing I got you that belt," said Woodica. "Now you can go looking like a proper princess."

"I don't want to go," muttered Roodica. "I'm happy with my own party."

The queen gave a deep sigh. "I'm afraid you won't be having your birthday party now, Roodica. The governor's party is on the same day and we have to go to it. We can't afford to upset the Romans."

"But what about my party? What about upsetting me?" cried Roodica

"I'm sorry," said the queen. "But there's nothing we can do."

"Nothing," sighed Foodica.

"Absolutely nothing," agreed Woodica.

"Rubbish," said Roodica. "There *is* something we can do."

"What?" asked her sisters.

"I don't know yet," said Roodica. "But I'll think of something. Just see if I don't."

The Romans Are
Superstitious

Roodica thought of something the very next morning during lessons with her teacher, Druid Big Brain.

"Today we're going to talk about the animals we see around us," he beamed at his pupils, who were sitting at the big table in the hall of Maiden Castle.

Roodica, who usually didn't like lessons, brightened up. "I could talk about Fleabag," she said. "He's the best dog in the world."

"I could talk about Frisky," said Gideon, the horse boy, and Roodica's best friend. "He's the best horse in the world."

"**Huh**, they're nothing compared to my dog and my horse," sniffed Copius Mucus, son of Fatius Guttus, the Roman tax collector, and Roodica's worst enemy. "Roman dogs and horses are so much faster and sleeker than your scruffy old bone sacks."

"Oh no, they're not!" yelled Roodica.

"Oh yes, they are," smirked Copius.

"Children, children," said Druid Big Brain. "We're not going to talk about domestic animals, but about the wild animals that live in the nearby forest."

"You mean like boars and bears?" said Roodica.

"And wolves," said Gideon.

"But not snakes," whined Copius. "I hate snakes. One fell from the roof of our villa this morning and slithered all the way across the courtyard."

Druid Big Brain eyed him keenly. "Ah, so that's why you're wearing an amulet today, Copius. I'd heard you Romans were very superstitious."

Copius fingered the lucky charm around his neck. "Yes, but pater says this will keep me safe."

"It won't keep you safe if a snake glides up your leg and bites your bum," giggled Roodica. "No matter what your father says." And she wiggled her arm at him. "Snakey snakey's coming to get you!"

"Stop it! Stop it!" cried Copius.

"That's quite enough, Princess Roodica."
Druid Big Brain was stern. "The Romans
take their superstitions
very seriously."

"Do they really?"
said Roodica, and
pulled down a
curl and chewed
it thoughtfully.

When lessons
were over Copius
rode home on his
fine stallion and Gideon went to tend
the horses in the settlement stockade.
Roodica stayed behind to have a word
with her teacher.

"Do you know any more about Roman superstitions?" she asked innocently. "They sound very interesting."

"Oh yes, they are," said Druid Big Brain, and he sat down and told her all he knew.

"Thank you," Roodica smiled when he'd finished. "I've learned a great deal. You keep a lot of things in that big brain, don't you?"

Druid Big Brain beamed and Roodica left him and set off for the stockade where Gideon was grooming his favourite horse, Frisky.

"Hi, Giddy up," she yelled. "Stop what you're doing right now. I need to talk to you. I have a brilliant idea and I need your help."

Gideon sighed. "Not another one. I'm not jumping out of a tree again to see if I can fly. Nearly broke my neck the last time."

"You looked more like a bear than a bird," agreed Roodica.

"And I'm not racing Fleabag across the river again, either."

"You were hopeless at the doggy paddle. Fleabag won easily. Anyway it's nothing like that. It's about my birthday party. You still want to come, don't you?"

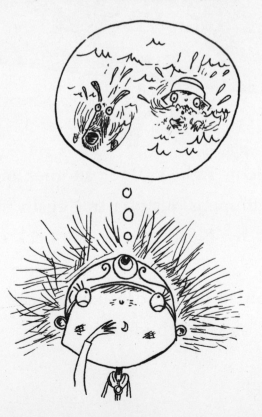

"Yes, but I thought it had been cancelled."

"Not if my brilliant idea works."

Gideon groaned. "But your brilliant ideas always get me into trouble."

"This one won't," grinned Roodica. "This one's really simple. I just need a black cat, some oil and a cockerel. Come on, we need to go and see Old Mother Silverlocks right now."

A Cat, a Cockerel and a Flask of Oil

Roodica and Gideon left the settlement and headed deep into the woods.

"I wonder why Old Mother Silverlocks doesn't live with the rest of us," said Roodica.

"It's because she's the wise woman. She knows about events before they happen and because she's really scary," muttered Gideon. "If you annoy her, she can turn you into things just by looking at you."

"What things?" Roodica was interested. "Could she turn me into a soldier so I could get a big sword and go off and fight the Romans?"

Gideon shook his head. "I don't know about that, but she can turn you into a frog or a toad or maybe even a tree." And he looked round fearfully. "Some of these trees could once have been people. The trunks seem to have eyes. Look!" He pointed at a gnarled old oak.

"Rubbish," said Roodica. "Those are just knots in the bark. You're more superstitious than the Romans. Old Mother Silverlocks can't turn you into anything."

"I wouldn't be *too* sure of that
Along with Midnight, my black cat
I can turn Gideon's knees to jelly
And set off butterflies in his belly . . ."

"I told you," yelped Gideon, and started shaking.

But Roodica looked around. "Where are you, Mother Silverlocks? I can't see you and I need your help."

Old Mother Silverlocks stepped out from behind a tree.

"I know why you've come to Mother
But one good turn deserves another
If my cat you wish to borrow
So you can give the Romans sorrow
You must help me with a task
That is not too much to ask."

"Of course not," grinned Roodica. "What do you want us to do?"

"I need wood to make a fire

Build my wood pile up much higher."

"Certainly," said Roodica, and she and Gideon set about collecting wood and carrying it to the cave where Old Mother Silverlocks lived.

When the wood pile was high enough Old Mother Silverlocks beckoned them into her cave.

"You go first," said Gideon.

Roodica laughed and went into the cave. Curled up in front of the fire was Midnight.

He looked up them and yawned. Old Mother Silverlocks picked him up and whispered in his ear:

"Go with Roodica and do your duty

Then return to me, my beauty."

Midnight miaowed, jumped down and stalked out of the cave.

"Thank you, Old Mother Silverlocks. I won't need him for long," said Roodica.

"What now?" asked Gideon, as the cat followed them back through the woods towards the settlement.

"Now we must go to see Saddler Sam. I need some of the oil he uses to oil the saddles."

Saddler Sam was outside his hut polishing a harness when they approached.

"Hi, Sam," said Roodica. "How are you?"

"Whatever you want, you're not getting it," said Sam, looking round. "Where's that hairy hound of yours. He's always knocking me over."

"He's not with me. I've got Midnight today instead."

"Midnight!" yelled Sam. "Old Mother Silverlocks's cat? Keep him away from me. He gives me the creeps."

"Then will you give me a little oil? I need it to upset the Romans."

Sam went into his hut and brought out a small flask. "Take it. Take it," he said and thrust it into her hand. "And take that cat away."

"Thanks, Sam," grinned Roodica. "Come on, Gideon. Come on, Midnight. Time to go and see Farmer Ned."

They found Farmer Ned in his barn forking up some hay.

"Hello, Farmer Ned," said Roodica. "I've come to ask a favour."

"Ah," said Farmer Ned. "Now you asking a favour usually means trouble for somebody."

"The Romans, I hope," grinned Roodica. "Especially Big Max, Fatius Guttus and Copius Mucus."

"That horrible lot," muttered Farmer Ned. "What is it you want?"

"I need to borrow your cockerel."

"Now what would you want Wakey Wakey for, I wonder?"

"He's part of my brilliant idea. With his help, I can have my birthday party with the settlement children instead of attending Big Max's party."

"Take him then, but mind you look after him and bring him back safely."

"I will," promised Roodica. "Gideon can catch him and carry him."

Why me?

Because you have to look after Wakey Wakey and Midnight till the party.

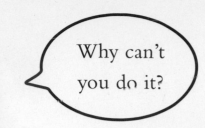

Why can't
you do it?

Because I'll be
looking after the oil. Bring
them to Big Max's villa at two
o'clock tomorrow. On the way
home I'll tell you what to
do with them . . .

Roodica, a Proper Princess?

Next day, Roodica got ready for Big Max's party.

Foodica could hardly believe it when Roodica asked her to fix her hair in the latest style.

"I never thought this would happen," she muttered, as she tamed the unruly hair.

Woodica could hardly believe it when Roodica put on her new dress and belt without a fuss.

"Am I dreaming this?" she muttered.

Fleabag rolled his big brown eyes when he saw Roodica in all her finery. He could hardly believe it. She didn't look like Roodica at all.

"You look very nice in the birthday presents your sisters have given you," smiled the queen. "Now here is one from me. It really *will* make you look like a proper princess." And she placed a beautiful gold torc around her youngest daughter's neck.

"Happy birthday, Roodica!"

"Happy birthday," echoed her sisters. "We're very sorry about your party. It's a real shame."

"Can't be helped," shrugged Roodica. "At least we've got the governor's birthday party to go to. I'll just get the chariot and drive us there."

"Why can't Gideon drive us?" frowned the queen.

"Er . . . I think he's got a problem with some of the animals." *Keeping Midnight and Wakey Wakey apart,* she thought to herself.

"Then mind you drive carefully," said the queen. "I don't want us arriving at the party covered in mud. What's that little flask for?" she added noticing the flask of oil Roodica had attached to her belt.

"It's for the . . . chariot wheels," Roodica crossed her fingers behind her back. "Sometimes they squeak a bit . . ."

Roodica hitched her pony, Plodette, up to the chariot and drove carefully down through the settlement.

"Happy birthday, Roodica," shouted all the children. "We're sorry about your party."

"I'm sorry too," said Roodica, and drove on.

Will, the blacksmith, stopped hammering for a moment. "Too bad about your party."

"Too bad," Roodica agreed.

Sam, looked from polishing a saddle. "I see you've got the oil. What did you say you wanted it for?"

But Roodica just waved and drove on quickly.

When they arrived at the large villa of Magnus Maximus, Roodica saw Copius Mucus and his father, Fatius Guttus, getting down from their splendid golden chariot.

"Don't park that broken-down set of wheels anywhere near us," ordered Copius. "I don't want it falling apart and causing damage. Take it round to the tradesman's entrance. That's where you Celts belong."

"Get out of my way before I run you over,

you snivelling, snotty, little slime bag.

"Roodica," said the queen sternly. "Remember you're a princess."

"Come along, Copius," said his father. "We're wasting good eating time. The governor always has plenty of delicious food at his parties." And he took Copius by the arm and waddled away.

Roodica found a space and parked the chariot. As they got out, she glanced around quickly.

"Looking for something?" asked the queen.

"Er . . . just admiring the garden," said Roodica.

"I'm glad to see you're taking an interest," said the queen. "Princesses should always take an interest in things."

"I could teach you all about herbs," said Foodica.

"I could teach you all about trees," said Woodica.

"Yes, good, spendid," smiled Roodica.

She had seen all she needed to see. The slightest flick of a black tail told her that Gideon was hiding in exactly the right spot with Midnight and Wakey Wakey.

She would be able to wave to him from the villa when the time was right. Her plan was in place. All she had to do now was put it into action.

Happy Birthday
to Who?

Roodica and her mother and sisters went up the fine marble steps to the governor's villa. Tall columns supported the roof and the large atrium was filled with people lining up to give their birthday gifts to the governor. Some gave big oil lamps, some gave bolts of silk. Fatius and Copius stood in front of Roodica with their gift; two large dogs which Copius held firmly by their leads.

"What have you brought to give Magnus Maximus?" he asked. "Some broken old pot, I expect."

"My mother and sisters have made a beautifully embroidered pillow filled with sweet herbs to help him sleep, Lottasnot," said Roodica.

"**Huh**, Celtic rubbish. We're giving him these magnificent guard dogs."

Roodica shrugged. "They look like wimps to me."

The guard dogs bared their teeth and snarled at her.

"Oh, go growl elsewhere," said Roodica. "You don't scare me."

The dogs strained on their leads and while Copius struggled to control them Roodica saw her chance to wave to Gideon.

"Who are you waving to?" Copius asked suspiciously.

"No one," said Roodica. "I think a bee was checking out my new hairstyle."

The line moved on and Fatius and Copius were just presenting their guard dogs to the governor when there was a gasp among the crowd. They all fell back as Midnight appeared. He strolled right up to the governor lazily flicking his tail from side to side.

"Oh no," said Magnus Maximus. "A black cat. That's a sign of bad luck. I hope it doesn't mean these dogs are going to bring me *bad luck*."

"Oh no, Governor," said
Fatius. "These dogs are
the finest money can buy.
They'll bring you *good luck*."
"And they'll soon make
short work of
the cat,"

laughed Copius, and he let them off the lead.

BIG MISTAKE.

Midnight arched his back, narrowed his eyes and gave a long, threatening **hisssssss** . . . The dogs looked wildly from side to side then took off . . . in the opposite direction.

"Come back! Come back!" yelled Copius. But it was no use, and the dogs soon disappeared out of sight.

"Great guard dogs," laughed Roodica.

And Midnight, his job done, strolled away.

Then it was their turn to present their gift. While the queen and her sisters handed over the pillow, Roodica secretly tipped some oil from her flask onto the floor beside the big oil lamps.

Then she moved forward. "Happy birthday, Governor," she smiled sweetly.

"I do hope you have a lovely day and please be careful not to slip on the oil that I've noticed leaking from those lamps. I think the dogs must have caused the spill as they ran past."

"What!" Magnus Maximus looked over at the puddle of oil. "That's another sign of bad luck. Fatius, this is all your fault. Have it cleaned up immediately."

"Oh I'm sure it wasn't . . . but . . . Copius, clean up the oil this minute!"

Roodica smiled sweetly as Copius scowled and got down on his hands and knees and, using the hem of his toga, started to wipe up the oil.

"I'm glad you spotted that, Princess Roodica," said the governor. "Very well done. Now if that's all the presents I'm getting, you may accompany me inside and the feasting can begin."

Oh no, thought Roodica, *how am I going to signal to Gideon if I'm stuck with the governor?*

But there was nothing else for it, she had to go inside. Her eyes opened wide when she saw all the food that had been laid out. There was fish, fruit, meat and sweetmeats of every kind. Enough to feed the settlement children for a fortnight.

Then she had an idea. "Governor, before I have something to eat, would you mind if I went back outside to help Copius clean up the oil. I'd like to make sure it's done properly."

The governor looked at her and smiled. "That's very kind of you, Roodica, you really are a proper princess."

Roodica smiled so sweetly her face started to ache, and she hurried outside. Copius was still mopping up the oil. Roodica crept up behind him and raised her hand to wave to Gideon. On its way back down, her hand may have slipped a little bit and clipped Copius on the head.

"Ow! What are you doing?"

"It was that bee again," said Roodica. "I thought I saw it on your head. Wouldn't want you getting stung. That would be *bad luck*." And she hurried back inside.

Everyone had started filling their platters with food. Fatius's was piled twice as high as everyone else's and he was just about to take his first mouthful when . . .

COCK A DOODLE DOO!

Wakey Wakey's cry rang out loud and clear.

"I don't believe it," cried Magnus Maximus. "A cockerel crowing! That's a sign of very, very bad luck, and on my birthday too. Everyone, stop eating RIGHT NOW!"

"What!" Fatius couldn't believe it either. The enormous piece of pie he was about to bite into had to be forced from his hand and put back onto the table.

"You may as well all go home now," said the governor. "The party's over. This has been a terrible day. But remember, because of that cockerel crowing, no Roman is allowed to eat anything else today or there will be even more bad luck."

Everyone turned to go except Fatius, who had to be dragged away from the table.

"This is all your fault." The governor poked him on his vast stomach. "If it hadn't been for you and those stupid dogs . . ."

"May I make a suggestion, Governor," said Roodica. "If no *Roman* can eat again today, may I take some of the food for the settlement children. It would be a

real treat for them and I shall tell them
of your kindness."

Magnus Maximus thought for a moment.
"Take it all," he said. "It'll only go to
waste otherwise. Perhaps giving it away
will help to change my luck."

"What about the birthday cake?"

"Take that too."

Roodica carried the cake while her
mother and sisters brought the rest of
the food.

Fatius and Copius watched hungrily as they piled it into their chariot.

"How did you manage it?" Copius scowled at Roodica.

"Manage what?" Roodica put on her most innocent look.

"To organise all that bad luck. I don't know how you did it, but I know you were behind it."

"Don't know what you're talking about," grinned Roodica. "That bee must have stung you on the brain. Or it would have, if you had one."

Roodica drove back extra carefully to Maiden Castle. She didn't want to damage the birthday cake. Gideon, Will, Sam, Druid Big Brain, Old Mother Silverlocks

and Farmer Ned were there to greet them,
as well as all the settlement children.

"What's everyone doing here?" asked
the queen.

"I think they've come to my birthday
party," grinned Roodica.

"But how did they know . . . ?"

Then the queen saw Midnight sitting
beside Old Mother Silverlocks and Wakey

Wakey tucked under Farmer Ned's arm. She looked at Roodica. "I see a black cat and a cockerel and I don't suppose there's much oil left in the flask on your belt."

"It may have leaked just a little bit . . ." grinned Roodica.

The queen smiled back. "I don't know what the settlement children would do without you, Roodica. Now let's get this food laid out and then we can have *your* birthday party."

"Right. I'll go and get changed."

"But you're dressed for a party already."

"But not a *kick-the-apple* party," grinned Roodica. "I promised the settlement children a kick-the-apple party and everyone knows proper princesses don't break their promises, and they certainly don't like to get their new clothes dirty ..."

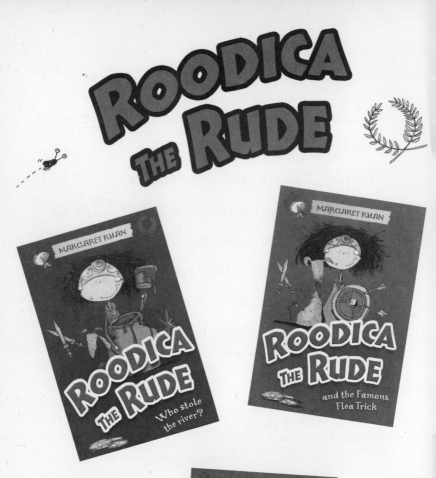

ROODICA THE RUDE

MARGARET RYAN

ROODICA THE RUDE
Who stole the river?

MARGARET RYAN

ROODICA THE RUDE
and the Famous Flea Trick

Collect them all!

MARGARET RYAN

ROODICA THE RUDE
and the Chariot Challenge